WELCOME, BABY!
Baby Rhymes for Baby Times

original rhymes by Stephanie Calmenson
pictures by Melissa Sweet

HarperCollinsPublishers

Welcome, Baby!

Text copyright © 2002 by Stephanie Calmenson

Illustrations copyright © 2002 by Melissa Sweet

"Barnyard Chat" originally appeared in *The Read-Aloud Treasury*,

published by Doubleday & Co., copyright © 1988. "What Babies Do," previously titled

"Babies," was published by Western Publishing Company, copyright © 1987.

Printed in Hong Kong. All rights reserved.

www.harperchildrens.com

Library of Congress Cataloging-in-Publication Data

Calmenson, Stephanie.

Welcome, baby! : baby rhymes for baby times / original rhymes by Stephanie Calmenson ;

pictures by Melissa Sweet.

p.   cm.

ISBN 0-688-17736-0 — ISBN 0-06-000492-4 (lib. bdg.)

1. Infants—Juvenile poetry.   2. Children's poetry, American.

[1. Babies—Poetry.   2. American poetry.]   I. Sweet, Melissa, ill.   II. Title.

PS3553.A425 W45   2002

811'.54—dc21   2001024634

CIP   AC

Typography by Stephanie Bart-Horvath

❖

1 2 3 4 5 6 7 8 9 10

First Edition

For Baby

Sing a song for baby.
Sing a song of joy.
We have a little girl!
We have a little boy!

Dance a dance for baby,
Happy as can be.
We have a brand-new baby.
We're a family!

Contents

Welcome, Baby!

Somebody special
Is due any day.
Everyone's happy because
Baby's on the way!

Let's make a baby blanket
With a pretty dove.
Knit one, purl one,
We'll put in lots of love.

Hear the needles going
Clickety-click.
See the blanket growing
Quickety-quick!

Knit one, purl one,
Mommy's glowing.
Knit one, purl one,
Baby's growing,
growing. . . .

Welcome, baby!
At last you are born.
We'll wrap you in your blanket
All cozy and warm.

Our baby has a blanket
With a pretty dove.
Knit one, purl one,
We put in lots of love.

Diaper Song

I see a baby
Whose diaper is wet.
I know how wet
A diaper can get.

Take the diaper off.
Wipe once. Wipe twice.
Sprinkle with powder.
That feels so nice.

Give a little tickle.
Sing a little song.
We changed your diaper.
It didn't take long.

Your Nose Knows

What does your nose know?

Your nose knows
It's got two eyes above it.

Your nose knows
It's got one mouth below it.

Your nose knows
It's got two ears beside it.

That's what your nose knows!

Barnyard Chat

"Honk, honk."
"Oink, oink."
"Meow, meow."
"Neigh."

"Cluck, cluck."
"Woof, woof."
"Gobble, gobble."
"Bray!"

"Baa, baa."
"Hoot, hoot!"
"Cackle, cackle."
"Moo."

"Quack, quack."
"Peep, peep."
"Cock-a-doodle-doo!"

Baby's Things

Here are some of baby's things:
Bottle, rattle, teething rings,
Rocking chair, teddy bear,
Clothes on hooks, lots of books,
Cuddly blanket, cozy crib,
Cup and spoon, pretty bib.
What other things do you see?
Can you say their names for me?

All Aboard!

Choo-choo!
All aboard!

Chugga, chugga,
Down the track.

Chugga, chugga,
Hurry back.

Choo-choo!
I love you-oo!

Who's a Good Baby?

Who's a good baby?
Who do you see?
Raise your arms and say,
"Me! Me! Me!"

What Babies Do

Look at what
These babies do.
Are these the things
That you do, too?

One little baby
Touches his nose.
Another baby
Wiggles her toes.

One baby laughs.
Another one cries.
This one plays peekaboo
And hides his eyes.
Peekaboo, kitten!

This baby crawls.
This baby stands.
This little baby
Claps her hands!
Can you clap, too?

Three hungry babies,
One messy face.
Now they go off
To have a race.
Look who wins!

It's time to get clean,
Rub-a-dub-dub.
This little baby
Plays in her tub.

All these babies
Like to play.
But why is one baby
Crawling away?

He needs to be changed.
He needs a big kiss.
Now he plays a game
That goes like this:

Pat-a-cake, pat-a-cake,
Baker's man!
Bake me a cake
As fast as you can.

There's one more thing
These babies do.
They wave good-bye.
Can you wave, too?

I Like Buttons!

Buttons here. Buttons there.
Some I push. Some I wear.

Push a button for the elevator.
Up or down I go!

Push buttons on the telephone.
Ring, ring, ring! "Hello!"

Buttons here. Buttons there.
Some I push. Some I wear.

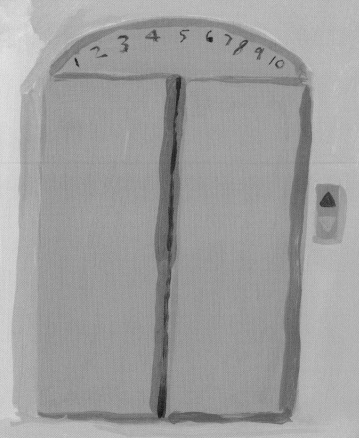

27

Messy!

For my hungry, hungry baby
Here are carrots, peas, and rice.
Here's some applesauce, too.
It tastes very nice!

A spoonful for my baby.
A spoonful on the floor.
A spoonful in your mouth,
But your chin has more.

Peas and carrots on the table!
Rice on the chair!
How did all the applesauce
Get in your hair?

Drink a little juice.
Blow a bubble or two.
You're my funny, messy baby
And I love you!

Splishy, Splashy

Splishy, splashy
In the tub.
Wet the soap,
Then scrub, scrub, scrub.

This is how
The washing goes:
Start at the head,
Then go down to the toes.

Wash the shoulders,
The belly, the knees.
When you get to the feet,
No tickling, please!

Little Blue Whale

Little blue whale
In a big blue sea,
Splish, splash,
Swim with me.
Dip a little,
Dive a little,
Dunk a little, whale.
Come back up
And flip your tail!

Here's My Ball

Here's my ball.
It's big and round.
I roll it, roll it
On the ground.
Roly, roly, poly!

Pots and spoons
Are very good toys.
I bang them together
And make lots of noise!
Bam-bam! Bam-bam!

I make bubbles
In the air.
Bubbles! Bubbles!
Everywhere.
Pop! Pop! Pop!

I have a truck.
I have a car.
I push or pull
And they go far.
Zoom! Zoom! Zoom!

Giddyap!

Come climb up
On Daddy's knee.
Take a horsey
Ride with me.

Giddyap! Giddyap!
Ride to town.
Giddyap! Giddyap!
Up and down.

Giddyap fast!
Giddyap slow.
Giddyap! Giddyap!
Giddyap! Whoa.

Silly Toe Song

Eyes and nose,
Mouth and TOES!

Ears and nose,
Mouth and TOES!

Cheeks and nose,
Mouth and TOES!

That is how this
Toe song GOES!

Babies in a Stroller

Babies in a stroller—
Roll him! Roll her!
We love to take a ride.
It's fun to be outside.

We count the cars and trucks.
We wave hello to ducks.
We put letters in the mail,
Pet a dog who wags her tail.

We smell a baker's pie,
Watch airplanes in the sky.
We get snacks to eat and then
We head for home again.

Babies in a stroller—
Roll him! Roll her!
We're sleepy from our ride.
It's time to go inside.

Peekaboo, Kangaroo!

Peekaboo,
Kangaroo,
Sitting next to
Baby's shoe.

Peekaboo,
Little cat,
Hiding under
Baby's hat.

Peekaboo,
Panda bear,
Are you cozy
On that chair?

Peekaboo,
Little mouse.
Are you hiding
In that house?

Peekaboo,
I see you,
Mouse and cat and
Panda bear, too.

Someone's missing!
Who can it be?
Turn the page.
Then you'll see.

Peekaboo,
Kangaroo!
You were hiding.
I found you!

Riding Shoulders

Riding shoulders way up high.
Waving to the passersby.
Grabbing glasses, grabbing hair.
Looking, looking, everywhere!
Riding shoulders way up high.
Up, up, up! Hello, sky!

Walking

Sit.
Crawl.
Stand.
Fall.

Stand.
Wobble.
Sway.
Bobble.

Bobble, bobble,
Stand. Stand.
Quick! Quick!
Hand! Hand!

Step, step!
Out of the way!
Walking, walking!
Hip, hip, hooray!

Talking

Ooh-ahh.
Baa-baa.
Ma-ma.
Da-da.

Up. Down.
Off. On.
No more.
All gone!

Clap hands.
Peekaboo!
So big.
I see you!

Bear. Oops!
Oh, my.
Go home.
Bye-bye!

Taking Care of Bear

I can take care
Of my very own bear.
What do I do?
Look, I'll show you.

Bear is hungry.
Needs to eat.
Feed him cereal.
It's a treat.

Bear is thirsty.
Pick him up.
Help him drink
From his cup.

Bear is happy.
Wants to play.
Roll the ball.
That's the way!

Bear is sleepy.
Needs to nap.
Rock him, rock him
In my lap.

Baby's Birthday

We're having a party!
Will you please come?
It's a special day—
Baby turns one!

We have boxes for baby
With presents inside.
Wrapping paper's fun.
We use it to hide.

Here comes the cake
With candle aglow.
We make a wish,
Then *huff-puff* we blow!

It's time to eat cake,
But before we do,
Let's sing to baby,
"Happy Birthday to You!"

A, B, C

A, B, C, D, E, F, G . . .
Say the alphabet with me.

H, I, J, K, L, M, N . . .
Keep on going, going, then . . .

O, P, Q, R, S, T, U . . .
You're almost done. Good for you!

V and W, X, Y, Z.
You said the alphabet with me!

1, 2, 3

1, 2, 3,
Count with me.

4, 5, 6,
We'll play no tricks.

7, 8, 9,
You're doing fine.

Look, here's 10.
Let's start again!

Red, Green, Yellow, Blue

Do you see a frog
With a hat on his head?
What color's the hat?
That's right. It's red!

Do you see a bird in
A bath getting clean?
What color's the bird?
That's right. It's green!

Do you see a bowl
That's filled with Jell-O?
What color's the Jell-O?
That's right. It's yellow!

Do you see a puppy
Whose leash is new?
What color's the leash?
That's right. It's blue!

Do you see red, green,
Yellow, and blue?
Can you point to the colors?
Can you name them, too?

Wiggle Your Fingers and Toes

Show me how you clap your hands:
    Clap, clap, clap!
Show me how you tap your feet:
    Tap, tap, tap!
Wiggle your fingers and toes!

Show me how you nod your head:
    Nod, nod, nod!
Show me how you flap your arms:
    Flap, flap, flap!
Wiggle your fingers and toes!

Clap your hands.
Tap your feet.
Nod your head.
Flap your arms.
Wiggle your fingers and toes!

Hug!

Who wants a hug?
Teddy Bear? Do you?
Yes, please!
Hug me, do!

Who else wants a hug?
Could it be pup?
One big hug
Coming right up.

Hug for cat.
Hug for mouse.
Lots of hugs
In this house.

Hug for sister.
Hug for brother.
Hug for father.
Hug for mother.

I think everyone
Likes a hug,
From a long-armed octopus
To a tiny bug.

Hugs feel good.
It's really true.
Are you ready?
This hug's for *you*!

Morning Walk

Daddy and baby
Woke early one day,
Buttoned their sweaters,
And went on their way.
They were quiet and didn't wake Mommy.

At Mr. Green's store
Across the street,
They bought sweet rolls
For a breakfast treat.
One of the rolls was for Mommy.

Next door there were flowers,
Pink, white, and blue.
What did Daddy
And baby do?
They picked a bouquet for Mommy.

They passed a tree
Where a small, blue bird
Sang the sweetest song
You ever heard.
They learned the song for Mommy.

Two gray squirrels
Just by chance,
Stopped to do
A happy dance.
They learned the steps for Mommy.

When they went back home
Mommy opened her eyes.
She saw all her presents.
What a happy surprise!

Then baby gave her
One more thing,
The very best present
A baby can bring—
A good-morning kiss for Mommy!

Windup Boy

Baby boy.
Windup toy.
Wind him up like so:

Turn the key.
Turn the key.
Now we let him go.

Go, baby! Go, baby!
Go, baby, go!

Grasshopper Girl

She's a grasshopper!
And we can't stop her!
Up from the grass she pops!
Then hop, hop-hop, hop-hops!

Sleepy Little Baby

Sleepy little baby.
Sleepy little town.
All the shops are
Shutting down.

Sleepy little baby.
Sleepy little street.
People going home
On tired feet.

Sleepy little baby.
Sleepy little house.
Everybody whisper
Quiet as a mouse.

Sleepy little baby.
Sleepy little bed.
Time to rest your
Sleepy little head.

Butterfly Kiss

A butterfly
Fluttered by
And gave a kiss
Just like this.

About the Author

Stephanie Calmenson loves to write for children. Her books have been called "marvelous" (*Publishers Weekly*), "lyrical" (*School Library Journal*), and "sweet, funny, and right on the mark" (ALA *Booklist*). Some of her most popular titles include DINNER AT THE PANDA PALACE, a **PBS** Storytime Book; THE PRINCIPAL'S NEW CLOTHES; THE FROG PRINCIPAL; THE TEENY TINY TEACHER; ROSIE, A VISITING DOG'S STORY; and GOOD FOR YOU! TODDLER RHYMES FOR TODDLER TIMES, which *School Library Journal* called a "winning collection."

Before becoming a writer, Stephanie was a teacher and a children's book editor. You can read more about the author at her website: www.stephaniecalmenson.com

About the Illustrator

Melissa Sweet has received universal praise for her "fetching watercolors" (ALA *Booklist*), "sunny art" (*The Bulletin of the Center for Children's Books*), and "delectable paintings" (*Publishers Weekly* starred review), which have appeared in Stephanie Calmenson's GOOD FOR YOU! TODDLER RHYMES FOR TODDLER TIMES; DIRTY LAUNDRY PILE: POEMS IN DIFFERENT VOICES, selected by Paul B. Janeczko; BOUNCING TIME, by Patricia Hubbell; WILL YOU TAKE CARE OF ME? by Margaret Park Bridges; and Kathi Appelt's BATS AROUND THE CLOCK, BATS ON PARADE, and BAT JAMBOREE.

Melissa lives with Mark, Emily, Arista, and a myriad of cats in Rockport, Maine.

Calmenson,
Stephanie.

Welcome, baby!

$18.89